Death Train

-OF-

≡ PROVINCETOWN ≡

Death Train
-OF-
PROVINCETOWN

TRENT PORTIGAL

radiant press

Book and cover design: Third Wolf Studio
Printed and bound in Canada at Friesens, Altona, MB

The publisher gratefully acknowledges the support
of Creative Saskatchewan and the Saskatchewan Arts Board.

Library and Archives Canada Cataloguing in Publication

Title: Death train of Provincetown / Trent Portigal.
Names: Portigal, Trent, author.
Identifiers: Canadiana (print) 20190090871 | Canadiana (ebook) 2019009088X |
ISBN 9781989274026
(softcover) | ISBN 9781989274040 (PDF)
Classification: LCC PS8631.O73825 D43 2019 | DDC C813/.6—dc23

radiant press

Box 33128 Cathedral PO
Regina, SK S4T 7X2
info@radiantpress.ca
www.radiantpress.ca

FOREWORD

THIS MODEST ESSAY is inspired by John Berger's *Art and Revolution*. His book was a critical intervention, pulling Ernst Neizvestny, a sculptor living at the time in the Soviet Union, out of obscurity. As I see it, Berger intended to begin a conversation about the inevitably political role of art, regardless of the intentions of the artist. It was a text to be written and "not to have written this essay would have been a form of cowardice and negligence."

I am not a critic of art or politics. My literary works, if I may call them that, are comprised of a handful of Provincetown tourist guides. *Virginia's Theological Cemetery: A Walking Tour* is perhaps the best known of them. Nonetheless, I have come across a couple of people who, like Neizvestny, deserve to be pulled from obscurity: the Virginia of the abovementioned cemetery and a sculptor who went by the Balzac-inspired name Mistigris.

My guides focus exclusively on people with headstones and other monuments to their lives. Here, I would like to write about two people who do not benefit from an obvious record of a life lived. The intent is not to build a grand historical monument to them, but to continue Berger's conversation.

1

VIRGINIA'S THEOLOGICAL CEMETERY: A WALKING TOUR, a guide book to one of Provincetown's most picturesque cultural landscapes, has been well received as a source of local history. It traces a route through the headstones and crypts, providing details peppered with pithy anecdotes of those interred there. It is a typical tour—what the Provincetown Cemetery Authority had asked for, and for which I was paid enough to spend some anxiety-free time writing these lines. In the middle of my research, I came across an obituary for Virginia that ended with "Virginia was a lewd degenerate for the glory of God." I knew then that there was a more important history to be told than the one I was writing.

Ironically, she was not laid to rest in her eponymous cemetery, so there was no good reason to dig further. Despite the laziness and impatience that have derailed my efforts to become a serious historian, further I went. I discovered two interconnected, equally fascinating worlds—that of Virginia herself, before she was reduced to the name adorning a cemetery gate, and that of the rail network built exclusively to transport the deceased and their loved ones to the city's cemeteries. I was taken in enough to contemplate writing an entirely different tour, for which I wrote a draft disclaimer before deciding better of it.

The disclaimer went something like this:

> When the cemetery opened, the tradition was to accompany the deceased to their final place of rest on foot. In order to simulate the experience, the government constructed a special train connecting the old cemeteries within the city limits to the new cemeteries needed to accommodate the growing population. This convenience allowed the new cemeteries to be located farther away—in this case, twenty kilometres from the city limits at the time. About fifty years ago, the line was dismantled. People had

come to prefer cars. In the spirit of authenticity, we will be walking the entire way to our destination. Please wear comfortable shoes.

As with the cemetery, little relating to Virginia's life was preserved in the city—a by-product of being labeled a "lewd degenerate," I suspect. One might have thought that the "glory of God" would counterbalance that label, but as you will learn later, the God in question was imported and didn't take on much of the local character. Several churches from Virginia's time still exist, but they have practically no connection to her. With no physical traces left, there is little point forcing people to walk all that way.

On the other hand, who wouldn't want to read about a lewd degenerate in the comfort of their own homes? Unfortunately for said readers, any salacious details would be pure fiction. No records of that nature—at least none that I could find—were ever kept. Besides, lewdness from a century ago would seem pretty tame today. Perhaps this absence of lurid detail is offset by the connection between Virginia's life and that of a certain joker sculptor named Mistigris.

2

I UNEARTHED THE FIRST mention of Virginia Antelme in a vice squad file from a raid—or perhaps an inspection—of an upscale brothel, a stone's throw from the seat of the regional council. The brothel was categorized as a 'house of tolerance', where prostitution was legally tolerated and regulated. Among other rules, prostitutes had to be registered and have medical checkups every six months. The primary concern was the spread of syphilis.

Virginia's name showed up several times over a three-year period as a member of the staff, which is to say that she was not a prostitute. It is unclear how the police made that distinction. If I were to speculate, they took the owner's word on it. Even the rumour of unclean girls would have driven clients elsewhere and run the risk of the authorities shutting it down. The risk was probably not worth the money saved on doctor's fees.

Virginia likely grew up in the countryside. From what is known about opportunities for women at the time, she probably migrated to the city as soon as she gained her independence. Like many others from the countryside, she would have had little education, had few skills of use in her new environment and come from a family without the means to help her find one of the more socially acceptable positions open to women, such as working in a store, clothing factory or as a domestic. In exchange for the freedom, she would do what she could to send money back home and help out the villagers who followed in her footsteps.

The house was frequented by regional councillors and their entourage, which gave the brothel the atmosphere of a gentleman's club. They followed the lead of the illustrious members of the Imperial government in the Capital. The councillors called themselves the Provincetown Players, a self-deprecating label that eventually became an ironic badge of pride. They knew that they played roles in a piece written in the Capital and that there was little chance they would ever leave their little theatre to join the production on the big stage. At the same time, Provincetown was their theatre and they were going to make the best of it. Their attitude translated into the demands they made on the places they frequented. As a result, the girls at the brothel were expected to display a certain level of education and decorum, so as to properly entertain and flatter their patrons. Although Virginia was not a prostitute, it is probable that she acquired a certain level of education there. That would help explain her evolution.

3

ACCORDING TO THE PLAYERS' correspondence, a significant number of policies and projects were determined at the house. It was there that they made the decision to create a Provincetown Academy of Fine Arts. It followed the model of the Capital, which, in turn, followed the French example. Art had been split rigidly into three areas: religious, academic and folk. Both religious and academic art were imported, so local art, regardless of the circumstances of its creation, could only be considered folk art.

The Players' ancestors were also imported. A couple of centuries earlier, the province's nobles had led a failed rebellion against the Empire. After their defeat, the nobles were exiled and their land confiscated. The vacuum was quickly filled with lesser aristocrats from the lands around the Capital, along with their religion. As the generations passed, a local identity developed. This emerging culture created a chasm between local customs and aspects of life tightly controlled by the Capital, including religion and art.

The sense of identity seemed to be defined by absence from the Capital and exclusion from Imperial affairs. Beyond that, the only real difference was the tendency to be "holier than the pope," as the saying goes. Mixing with the "folk" culture around them, beyond what was necessary to impose their own values, was unthinkable. The girls at the brothel were acceptable because they adapted to the Players' values. Local artists who espoused academic principles could also play a role, but only once an institution was established that clearly differentiated their work from folk art. Everyone else was just background, there to add colour to the scene. Nobody was labeled a moral degenerate, as that would have lent them more importance.

4

THE OTHER MAJOR PROJECT developed at the house was a literal example of being holier than the pope. The Players decided to take more seriously the notion of people being equal in death. Burial practices, up until that point, had been to offer an effectively permanent lease on plots large enough for crypts and other significant monuments for the richest. The well-off could lease more modest casket-sized plots with space between them for up to thirty years. The lower classes had the option of leasing plots with no space between them for up to ten years. The poorest were relegated to common graves, where bodies were stacked.

The initial idea was to allow everyone to be buried with space between them in permanent plots. After learning that graveside visits tapered off completely in under twenty-five years in the vast majority of cases and that the land needed for permanent graves was more significant than they imagined, a more modest policy was enacted. All new plots needed to be a minimum of half a casket-width and half a casket-length apart. The minimum lease was set at twenty years, with subsidies available for the poor. Much later, people gave a great deal of credit for this initiative to Virginia. She did not bother correcting them.

Provincetown's living poor were for the most part stacked in crowded tenements. The houses were concentrated in tortuous, segregated neighbourhoods. Though this world and that of the Players seemingly shared the same religion and were exposed to the same religious art, they attended services at different churches. The services were led by clerics trained in the same seminaries clustered around the Capital, but they adapted themselves to the expectations of their audiences. In a way, the only neighbourhood the two worlds shared was the cemetery.

5

THE PLAYERS' FIXATION on the genteel, academic values of those with whom they shared their stage, and on their absentee aristocratic audience in the Capital, was their downfall. They didn't realize until it was too late that the whole world was being rebuilt around them, with new stages demanding new local audiences at an ever-accelerating pace.

As with everywhere else, the railroad was the biggest driver of change. The Players were not ignorant of this. They simply did not have a thorough understanding of Provincetown. They made several erroneous assumptions, the most important of which was that people in and around Provincetown without opportunities or links to the community would tend to move to the Capital. The town, they imagined, would become more homogenous and easier to govern.

They were not totally wrong; for the majority of people, the Capital was the most attractive destination. However, a significant number preferred Provincetown. This group sought the business opportunities of a city but were horrified by what they saw as the degradation and decadence of urban life. These were the sorts of people who would not hesitate in labeling Virginia as a moral degenerate and found it difficult to ignore poor neighbourhoods, houses of tolerance and similar closed worlds.

These people intended to change Provincetown for the better, both economically and morally. Concerned with the effects of weak social ties on other people's children, they pushed for the state to step in. They considered their own children to be above reproach but still vulnerable to bad influences in the urban environment. With the clout resulting from the success of their newly established factories and the support of religious leaders, they brought about sex education in schools. It is hard to imagine today that sex education was originally a conservative initiative, but that is how it started.

Education was controlled by the Capital. The Players were not invited to give an opinion on the matter. The success of the initiative shifted the social norms of Provincetown. The private stage of the house of tolerance was no longer the appropriate venue for politics. Decisions had to be made in view of those who represented the rising economic power in the city and be buffered as much as possible from vice.

Houses of tolerance continued to exist for a certain time, but only where syphilis and other venereal diseases could cause significant economic disruptions. The same burgeoning industrialists behind sex education ensured that houses were allowed in proximity to their factories. Those around barracks were also encouraged. They were just no longer acceptable for the elites of local society.

When the houses of tolerance finally disappeared completely, it was because prostitution was no longer considered a social activity. Some of the old buildings, however, still exist and could make for an interesting tour.

6

THE MIGRATION TO THE CAPITAL also had an influence on Provincetown. Urban blight was becoming too widespread to ignore. The breaking point was a three-month long period of unrest the Empire blamed on foreign provocation. There is no evidence backing the claim. Most sources point to a spike in food prices, but one does not exclude the other.

Regardless, an initiative was launched in the name of public health once calm had been restored, christened the Light and Air Program. Streets were widened, dilapidated buildings were torn down, and hills were leveled. Sidewalks, boulevards and parks were constructed. Better quality yet ultimately unsound housing was built. Sewer, gas and water lines were installed.

There is a record of smallpox and cholera outbreaks in poor neighbourhoods. The government insisted that the program was intended to address the outbreaks and was not a response to the period of unrest. Evidence suggests however that there was little differentiation between disease and certain groups of people in the minds of the decision makers. Cleaning up a neighbourhood would optimally take care of both.

In order to keep the entire Empire healthy or pacified, depending on which version you believe, the Capital exported the program to other major centres, including Provincetown. The initiative put a spotlight on areas of the city the Players had chosen to ignore. The council also inherited the headache of dealing with people displaced by the work. The messiness of the situation caused several Players to withdraw from politics, to be replaced by figures from the sex education campaign who wanted to solidify their newfound influence.

7

VIRGINIA ADAPTED. Anecdotes from letters she later sent to Violet Mascolo, of Violet's Deontological Necropolis, indicate that she landed as a server in a bar in a middle class neighbourhood. Servers at the time functioned more like subcontractors than employees; they bought drinks from the owner and sold them to clients for whatever price they could get. If they were sufficiently charming, they could convince the client to buy them drinks. The owner would sell the servers a counterfeit drink for much less money, and the servers in turn would pocket the difference. Prostitution in the establishments was illegal but tacitly encouraged. Some bars had rooms discretely hidden in the back or in nearby buildings.

Although the neighbourhood was not heavily impacted by the Light and Air Program, a proper sidewalk was constructed during Virginia's time there. Women could not enter the bars without compromising their virtue, but they could order drinks without going in during daylight hours. Owners recognized the opportunity the sidewalk presented and quickly claimed a portion of it with chairs and tables.

Servers rarely ventured out to the sidewalk. Their appearance was seen to undermine the respectability of the establishment. The women who sat at the sidewalk tables were also considered less susceptible to their charms than the male patrons, so the servers' talents would be wasted. Finally, they were generally not able to deal with the aggressive street prostitutes and other undesirables the sidewalk attracted.

In a letter, Virginia mused about whether the respectable Violet had only been a windowpane away years before they actually met. She did not give an indication as to whether she sold more than drinks.

8

ABOUT A DOZEN BLOCKS away from where Virginia worked, in a poor quarter half-demolished to make way for the Light and Air Program, the joker sculptor Mistigris was born. It turned out people were more resilient than diseases. As with Virginia, there are few records on his early life. I am tempted to say that the best description of the world he inherited was from the poetry of the dandies and flâneurs who wandered around dying neighbourhoods before all traces of them were lost, romanticizing the tortuous streets and tenements with attempts at verse. These literary passages are undoubtedly connected to my temptation to romanticize Mistigris himself. Provincetown, however, was not Paris.

His childhood was spent in a hastily built utilitarian world, with utility defined as a narrow notion of wellbeing. Housing had all the basic modern amenities. Streets were large enough to provide air and light. Parks fitted out with equipment to improve the body were conveniently located. While the development lacked character, it was in fact better in almost every way than the slum housing it replaced.

New construction techniques allowed the buildings to go up to six or even eight stories, double what was there before. The extra height provided sufficient space and low enough prices for most people to stay. It was only the most marginalized, the people the Players most wanted to ignore, that they had to figure out what to do with. It dawned on the councillors that these new parks and sidewalks were themselves prominent stages and it would not do to have undesirables cluttering them up.

Mistigris did not grow up in the bland environment envisioned by the Program, but one where premature decay was increasingly visible through the thin veneer of modern comfort. The budget for the program was fixed in advance. For it to be implemented, private land had to be expropriated. The government set up local boards to determine the fair value to compensate landowners. The boards were made up of notable people who tended to be landowners. They drove up the price over time. As a result, there was less money for construction and corners were cut. Our joker sculptor would have seen fresh, new buildings rise from the rubble just to witness them fall into an inescapable spiral of decline. Critics of his art often use "decay" and "decline" when describing its central themes.

9

THE ACADEMY OF FINE ARTS set up by the Players survived the shift, but was challenged by an artists' union. The union was closely linked to the rising industrial and banking powers and aimed to represent their values. As with the push for sex education, its values were ultimately conservative. It was not a question of introducing formal art education to compensate for the lack of informal mores in the city. The only art available in the morally upright countryside was religious, which was already well represented in the city by religious leaders. The union's role was to keep the tradition of academic art intact while giving the industrialists the prestige of guiding it.

The subjects and styles of the art did not significantly change. What did change were the materials. Artists were encouraged to use supplies over which the industrialists had a virtual monopoly. Requests for supplies could only be made through the union. The physical substance of art took on a new importance for the select few. For most people, art remained intangible and abstracted from ordinary life.

The Light and Air Program created a conflict between artists and business in the union. Classically, artists were commissioned to enrich new buildings with sculptures and paintings. Art was integral to architectural design. The industry behind the union was heavily involved with the neighbourhood reconstruction, as well as with driving up the value of expropriated lands. When it became clear that the designs were stripped of all detail to save costs, the artists protested noisily.

The developers argued that housing and shops for the sort of people who would live there were always simple and plain. The only art that such people appreciated outside churches was crude folk art and it would not do for the highly respected artists of Provincetown to lower themselves to that level. Besides, the money saved could go toward transforming the hall, where the yearly art exhibition was held, into a palace. The union came to an agreement that, so long as artists were involved in the design of the palace, it could accept being uninvolved in poor neighbourhoods.

10

VIRGINIA WAS LISTED in police records roughly a year after she became a server. According to the file, she was involved in an altercation involving a patron's wife. Ignoring the unspoken rules governing when unaccompanied respectable women may be out on the sidewalks—especially in proximity to bars—the woman spotted her husband being charmed by Virginia. Even though the bar had windows, they were covered in a manner that let light pass while making it difficult to see in. It is doubtful that the wife came across the scene by accident.

Virginia later briefly described what happened. She was particularly impressed with the wife's use of a chair to prolong the conflict long enough for the police to intervene. The woman did not cause as much damage as she could have, as she wavered between attacking the servers and smashing the bottles of alcohol behind the bar. She loudly blamed both for the moral corruption of her husband. The owner came out with the worst injuries, having broken several bones in his hand after trying and failing to grab the chair.

Incidents like this were not uncommon, though they seemed to end more in tears than in violence. Alcohol and easy women, it was felt, were irresistible sirens to men. Better explanations that took into account how society was organized were suggested in fiction, academia and the occasional newspaper article, but they had little impact.

Virginia would likely not have noted the incident in a letter if it had not led to an interesting conversation among the servers. They agreed that the rooms in the back were disgusting. Clients generally avoided them unless they were very drunk. The servers did not insist, since they despised them just as much. The bar owner's only suggestion was that the servers take on cleaning duties. Some of them made an effort, but shifts were too long and simply too exhausting to do it regularly. As a result, servers went further with their charms in the main room than they would have liked. This made incidents especially awkward.

The conversation gave Virginia the idea to rent a couple of rooms in a building down the street and let certain of the servers know. The servers were non-committal at first, but after being able to entice clients who would never use the bar's back rooms, they warmed up to the suggestion. She did not remark on how she was able to pay the first months' rent and furnish the rooms.

11

WE DO KNOW SHE HIRED a young woman named Louise as a maid and general gopher. Looking to broader trends rather than actual evidence, it's possible to guess Louise came from the same village as Virginia. It would have fallen to Virginia, as the first from the village to successfully establish herself in the city, to help those who came after. It is practically unthinkable that she included details on exactly what she was doing in Provincetown that enabled her to send money back home. Lacking connections to the world of socially acceptable work, she would have had little choice but to hire Louise to ensure her specific duties at the very least were respectable.

Though her correspondence never mentioned the Players' house of tolerance, it was likely her experience there that made her plan a success. The rooms fulfilled both the desire of the newly rich to take on the trappings of the aristocracy while being sensitive to their sexual prudishness. The rooms gave them an intimate stage and a captive audience to play their physical virility. Afterward, they could join the cast on the sidewalk to play their moral superiority, even if just for the time it took to cross it and get into a vehicle.

The owner of the bar was reportedly displeased to be left out of the arrangement. He accepted it nonetheless because the drop in incidents and connection to higher quality rooms gave the establishment more respectability. Though clients were drinking less, he could charge more. Sometime later, he was also able to turn the back rooms into a stage large enough to accommodate a modest chorus line. As Provincetown became more affluent, entertainment options diversified. Going to a show was more dignified and decent than drinking, at least on the surface.

12

THOUSANDS OF INDIVIDUALLY insignificant villagers like Louise formed a wave of migration that overfilled the sidewalks, resulting in a new level of conflict. The regional council, an odd mixture of old Players and new councillors who rarely agreed on anything, managed to come to a consensus on the need for a visible police presence. Poverty was overwhelming the scene and needed to be kept in check.

Street prostitution did not disappear. The prostitutes quickly learned that police did not have any power in private passageways and malls, and private security was generally lax. So, the girls stayed in proximity to these no-man's areas. If cops became aggressive, they would make as big a scene as possible. Since the point of the police was to reduce discord in public, officers who were seen as causing commotions did not last long.

Young women were frequently the victim of this policing because they were easy targets. They did not have the self-assurance to impose themselves on this chaotic stage. Men, ever more confident and self-assured, regularly accosted them if they were unaccompanied. It was simpler for a policeman to deal with them than the men, so officers made it clear that the sidewalks were off-limits outside of specific hours.

Along with policing came flashy, colourful graffiti. Poor people and loitering children were told forcefully to move on. The creative and stubborn ones figured out that it was possible to claim the space without being physically there and taking a beating for it. The more serious artists also liked that the walls of the middle-class areas were not crumbling like the buildings in the neighbourhoods they tended to live in. While the police did reduce some conflicts, they only managed to transform a great many of them.

13

VIRGINIA OCCASIONALLY SPENT afternoons on a bench in a park in the poor neighbourhood a dozen blocks from the bar. Most street conflict happened where people wanted to be seen, so the trick to being left in peace in public was finding a place with an unappreciative audience. The space was mostly taken up by young children and mothers. The mothers occupied themselves with sufficiently portable housework, such as sewing and knitting, while the children used up their excess energy.

One day, a woman far too respectable to be in the park sat beside her. The woman, named Violet, gazed at the children and spontaneously started in on a monologue about how she had always thought that being a mother would change everything, but that she was mistaken. She continued, saying that a loveless marriage stayed loveless. A penny-pinching, distant husband did not suddenly become generous or attentive. A barren and uncomfortable house was still not a home. Virginia wrote later that the speech was remarkable for how off-putting it was to a perfect stranger.

After some reflection, Virginia realized that she had heard far more about domestic life from men than from women. Married clients could be split into two categories: those who pretended their home life did not exist and those who endlessly complained about it. She knew the second group was trying to rationalize their behaviour, mainly to themselves. Still, over time, she internalized some of what they were saying. She decided to spend more time on the bench.

As the monologue evolved into dialogue, Virginia not only discovered a new side of married life, but also one of prostitution. Violet described how her husband, and many like him, tightly controlled family finances. He would happily spend lavishly on mistresses, all the while refusing his wife anything more than the bare necessities. Many women found that becoming mistresses in their own right was the only way to accumulate money they could freely spend. Violet was as vague as Virginia as to whether she was one of these women.

One difficulty was in finding discreet places for these trysts. Virginia, at that moment open to new opportunities, offered her rooms. After some hesitation, Violet offered her connections in society and the two found themselves in business together.

14

ACROSS THE CITY, in a seemingly identical neighbourhood, at around the same time the two women first met, Mistigris was sitting on a copy of the same bench. According to the one retrospective of his work that has been written, he was watching the rubble of a collapsed building. He had been one of the first on the scene, helping dig people out as best he could. When he, in turn, collapsed from exhaustion, someone helped him to the bench. White with concrete dust, he saw the hope of finding survivors slowly fade away and laughed. Records show that twenty-three people died, although none were closely connected to the sculptor. The retrospective likely made the scene out to be more dramatic than it was.

Tragedy and spectacle gave Mistigris the motivation to create publicly. He started as a graffiti artist. Unlike his peers, who were primarily interested in claiming space as their own, Mistigris wanted to spread symbols of decline and decay, especially on surfaces that seemed indestructible and unchanging. Others chose high-profile locations, though what was high-profile to them was often different than, say, the Players. Stages and audiences overlapped imperfectly. Mistigris painted in seemingly random places in public, but without a clear audience.

Some have read into this work a critique of the supposedly eternal Empire. Mistigris, however, never expressed any political motivation. Artists of the era made a habit of writing and signing manifestos. Even Academy and union artists felt the need to support their practice with public declarations. They had to explain how they were socially engaged by creating art largely irrelevant to the world around them. Throughout his career, Mistigris wavered between claiming that Provincetown was his house, with art being a sort of backyard hobby, and assuming the pose of the detached, aloof artist who refused to be tied down to domestic trappings such as a formal community. He was labelled an anarchist.

15

ONCE THE STAGE was constructed, the bar was transformed into a concert hall initially named Subeline. Concert halls were more respectable than bars. To be successful though, halls needed to attract a different kind of audience. The newly rich were evolving into a demanding leisure class. They relied on others to provide distractions from their bleak home lives, and the spectacle on stage quickly proved necessary but still inadequate. Every aspect of the hall needed to entertain.

Artists and pseudo-bohemians were encouraged to spend their evenings there. Unless they started to overwhelm the place, drinks were cheap and the show was free. Academy and union artists, more restrained and financially better off, were less interested by the offer. The pseudo-bohemians were really not much more interesting. Their reputation for being entertaining tended to colour how they were seen.

The entertainers on stage were popular but generally not well compensated. Predominantly women, they were poorly paid and responsible for the costs of costumes and everything else needed for the show. Without passion, there was no reason to perform, and without talent, there was no way to continue. They were ultimately in a more difficult position than the servers—the vast majority were also prostitutes in one form or another. The most successful were mistresses to men who could offer them long-term security but did not demand exclusivity.

The best had apartments. For others, Virginia offered rooms. She wrote to Violet with apparent fascination how the fantasies of the stage were translated in the bedroom. Anecdotes quickly turned into requests for room embellishments, and she was happy to accommodate them. The days of generic aristocratic luxury were ending.

Violet responded angrily whenever Virginia described new

extravagances. There was only so much money to go around, and the wives always suffered when more was spent on other women. She did recognize, though, that it was good for business.

16

THE ADDED BUSINESS from the respectable women of Violet's world and entertainers led to an increase in the number and variety of rooms available. Virginia made connections in the hall with artists, both of the crafts and fine arts variety. She offered those interested opportunities to put their touches on the rooms. She appreciated their imagination but was under no illusion about what was important. Clients were more excited about the idea of artistic touches than the nuance of the designs. At the same time, sexual excitement still trumped everything else. Nothing could be too off-putting or distracting.

The caretaking staff grew from Louise to a small army. Virginia only mentioned staffing issues with Violet obliquely. She also preferred hiring people informally, so no official records exist. The choice had less to do with the nature of the business, which was not explicitly against the law, than the fact that she employed mainly women. Most jobs were closed to women and the others were not typically considered respectable. "Whore" was used not only to describe women who sold their bodies, but also those who worked in the service industry and so were in the position to tempt men.

At about that time, Louise returned to her village. The government had become concerned at the large numbers of young people migrating to the city. Farms were usually handed down from generation to generation. Family farms were being bought by industrial farmers in certain locations, but in others a lack of interested heirs could be a significant problem. If enough farms stopped operating, even for a short time, food prices would rise, leading to social unrest. The government passed a series of amendments to avoid the crisis. One was to allow women to inherit, and therefore become owners of, farmland. Louise intended to take advantage of the change.

Violet suggested that she and Virginia do the same. The drafters of the law did not consider the possibility that women could have the means to purchase land outright. It did however limit ownership to unmarried women of age. If the woman married, the land would pass to her husband. Virginia promised that if Violet found suitable land, she would buy enough for both of them. They dreamed of offering clients cabins to fulfill fantasies of rural simplicity.

They purchased land to the north and south of Provincetown, but they soon found the demands of installing modern luxuries in cabins, securing reliable transportation and other details to be too much of a challenge. Instead, they leased the land to neighbouring farmers who wanted to expand but didn't have the capital to buy it themselves.

17

THE LIGHT AND AIR PROGRAM came to an end at that point. It turned out that tax revenue from the improved properties would cover the costs within a decade. Despite this, the government did not want to take on another project of a similar scale. They did however want to maintain their visibility across the Empire. Among their initiatives was to fill sidewalks and parks with statues, later broadened to sculptures.

In Provincetown, calls for art were generally open, but the program was managed by the Academy and the union, with the union jurying submissions. Artists chosen were inevitably members of one or both organisations, which occasionally led to conflict of interest accusations. The conflict was explained away by criteria of quality, style and subject. The government had certain expectations and the only reason artists would not be members of the organizations was if they did not conform to them.

Mistigris regularly submitted proposals, despite his lack of membership. None were accepted. They were, however, the first indication of his move from painting to sculpture. He focused on metal, twisting the subject in ways that kept it recognizable while introducing unmistakeable signs of decay and decline. It was a clear case of following the letter of the calls while flouting their spirit.

The winning sculptures were—and continue to be—grandiose. They straightforwardly celebrated the Empire through scenes, events and individuals. Nothing in these works hinted at Provincetown's unique identity. People on sidewalks and in other public places found themselves outclassed by objects larger than life. The government claimed that the works provided the masses with 'moral uplift'—permanent models for what to strive for in life. They were obvious targets for graffiti, public urination, and other unintended uses.

If you are interested in learning more about these works, I highly recommend the lovely walking tour by Genestas. His guide does justice to their transition from representing Imperial glory to their reduced status as nostalgic tourist attractions as the Empire transformed into a modern nation state.

18

THE LAST MAJOR INITIATIVE that can be attributed to the old Players was the establishment of two new cemeteries outside the limits of Provincetown and the train that linked them to the city. The Capital was experiencing another in a long list of crises. Rapid population growth from migration had resulted not only in housing problems for the living, but also for the dead. Their established cemeteries were full and they were scrambling to find appropriate land for new ones.

While Provincetown did not have the same level of migration, the Players' decision to treat people as equals in death if not in life meant that more cemetery space was used per person than anywhere else in the Empire. As a result, the two cities faced the same problem at roughly the same moment.

The challenge for both Provincetown and the Capital was location. Traditionally, people walked with the casket from home to the church and from the church to the cemetery. At the risk of causing social unrest, the cemetery could not be too far from the city. Opposing this were public health concerns: if the cemetery was located in the same basin as people's drinking water, the water could be contaminated. Water treatment was not widely used. Cities were built around basins, so being in the next basin meant being farther away.

A third consideration was cost. The closer the land was to the city, the more expensive it was. There was also no appetite or budget to expropriate land after the experience of the Light and Air Program. The government and the Provincetown regional council had to find willing sellers. Some people in government cursed the passing of the law that allowed women to own land, since it made farmers less willing to give up family holdings.

Several bureaucrats in the Capital came up with a solution to the conflicting considerations. If a train was built between existing cemeteries and new ones, distance would cease to be an issue. Mourners could follow their tradition by walking to an old cemetery, and then board a train to take them to the new one. The new one would be located in the next valley, wherever some landowner would give up the land for a reasonable price.

The train would have to be used exclusively for transit between cemeteries. Mixing mourners and other passengers on a regular line would be disrespectful to God and the deceased. It would also be awkward for everyone else. Since there were no other reasons to travel between cemeteries that they could think of, the track would end up being exclusive as well.

This solution was too significant a development and too much like the new roads of the Light and Air Program to be palatable in the Capital, but the Provincetown Players saw the idea and the inability of the government to implement it as another opportunity to show that Provincetown was more advanced than the Capital.

Industrialists on the regional council had excess capacity since the Light and Air Program had wound down and were willing to trade a certain amount of profit for prestige. Routes were available out of the city, through land already expropriated that was still owned by the government and the underground freight tunnels that led to the central market. All that was needed was to find land for the new cemeteries.

19

IN A SCENE REMINISCENT of the house of tolerance, most of the discussions took place in the concert hall where Virginia worked. She was no longer a maid though, and did not hesitate to offer the land she had bought for herself and Violet. She did not offer to sell it, but suggested that the council could take over the leases from the farmers.

The leasing option was a revelation for the councillors in the hall. Up until that point they assumed that they had to purchase the land. Without that burden, ample money would be available for the train. Given how Virginia described the discussion, one wonders what corners they might have cut to do both. The train might have derailed and exploded in the middle of the city, causing countless deaths with no way of getting them to their final resting place. The councillors were also attracted to the practicality of having land on two sides of the city.

Violet was enthusiastic, since a council lease afforded them more long-term stability. She joked that they would finally have a place for the necrophilia fetishists. Ultimately, after the first flash of interest in owning farmland, neither woman wanted to put more effort into dealing with the land than necessary.

The names "Virginia's Theological Cemetery" and "Violet's Deontological Necropolis" were used in the original lease. There were no reasons given for the choice. If I were to speculate, I would say that the lease was drawn up in the hall and that a pseudo-bohemian suggested them. It is the only official record of Violet's name I have come across in relation to her business with Virginia.

Some readers may recall the cemeteries were initially named after saints. A petition to the regional council a dozen years ago triggered the change to what it claimed were the "original names." The decision was far from unanimous.

20

AS A LABEL, "ANARCHIST" was used to describe a variety of people who often had little in common. From an artistic standpoint, defacing property was a shared starting point. If respectable people could easily figure out the point of the graffiti or equivalent, it was put into the appropriate category. Whatever was left over was anarchy. Advertising, marking of territory, and folk art were the most common categories.

Anarchist artists could be roughly split into two groups. The first was consciously politically active and the second tended to avoid politics. The line between them wasn't clear. For instance, simply walking along one of the newly built sidewalks could be seen as a political act. Manifestos give us a useful criterion, but in no way can they be considered definitive. Mistigris was not intentionally political. Beyond avoiding manifestos, we have accounts of groups attempting without success to set him and his work up as part of their program or as an enemy to it. Everyone felt that the themes of decay and decline were obvious and powerful. Mistigris' work was visible to a larger public than the typical academic works, more often than not easel paintings. It also gave a sense of society's movement, missing in official art, that could support reforms across the political spectrum.

On one side, it was a symbol of the continuing moral decay of the city. Authority needed to be reinforced so the legacy of the sculpted heroes of the Empire could live on. On the other, the lethargy of the Empire was increasingly obvious. The system could not keep up with the pace of modern life and so needed to be reformed or replaced.

The informal connections in his neighbourhood and the broader city were all Mistigris cared about. He needed help to shift some of his larger pieces in his cramped studio, just to continue to create. If a piece made its way to the outside world, even more hands were required. As a sculptor whose work sometimes reached monolithic proportions, it was impossible to be an aloof, isolated artist.

21

THE CONTRACEPTION CONTROVERSY, in which practically everyone felt the need to take a side, tested the resolve of the apolitical. It began when several highly respected doctors at the university hospital in the Capital wrote an open letter to the government. They argued that contraception should be legalized and made easily available to everyone on both human suffering and financial grounds. The letter was the result of years of frustration and ethical unease, one of the signatories explained later.

The specialists who signed the pro-contraceptives letter effectively dropped a bomb. The reaction was hostile, making the act counter-productive. People who discreetly provided services for the most vulnerable scattered with the noise and light of the explosion. It was as if the doctors thought of themselves as noble heroes, in the mold of the statues spread around the Empire's cities. Instead of attracting support for their cause, though, they became a target of derision and mocking graffiti.

The girls in the concert hall did not talk politics unless clients wanted to. Living and working in a hidden world of moral decline and being seen by much of society as one of the reasons for that decline, they felt disconnected from politics. It was lines they had to be prepared to speak as part of their performance.

Clients discussed politics amongst themselves as if it was a sport. They felt freer in the hall to speculate on strategies, teams and individual players. The context was important, as it gave them a sense of being a spectator rather than being in the middle of the fray. The girls, pseudo-bohemians, and others were part of the context. If anything, their role was not to contribute ideas, but to tease them out of the politicians and industrialists. Virginia's forwardness with the cemeteries was unusual.

The contraception controversy flipped the situation. Suddenly, the clients felt uncomfortable expressing their ideas in the hall and many of the girls considered themselves personally implicated. The former simply avoided the subject and the latter still played their role. The pseudo-bohemians were the only ones to bring it up, taking positions hostile to use and availability.

Everyone was aware that industrialists with large work forces spoke against contraception in public but encouraged it in their factories. They knew that religious and political leaders on the big stage of the Capital were against it. Many were aware that politically active anarchists were for it and that the medical community was split down the middle.

Virginia initially tried to stay above the conflict. The letter opened the floodgates for the girls of the hall. Most were already using one form or another when possible, but they were discreet about it. After the letter, when they were not putting on the show, they started to discuss techniques and tactics openly.

The respectable ladies who used Virginia's rooms acted like their husbands. They were vocal about their opposition, but were more pragmatic in practice. What was clear was that neither group wanted to be associated with someone openly contrary to their views. Both Virginia and Violet had strong opinions, but both decided that it would be bad for business to say anything. Even in their letters, their positions were ambiguous.

22

SOME OF THE YOUNGER GIRLS looked to Virginia for guidance and support. She was willing to help insofar as it kept her business running smoothly and steered them away from scandal. In a letter to Violet, she actually brought up Mistigris as a cautionary tale. It was all well and good to focus on the decay, moral and otherwise, of society. Getting so close as to lose all perspective was a guaranteed way to become a pariah. Her point of view had more in common with the industrialists than the servers.

She did not help girls with abortions, venereal diseases or any of the other hazards of their activity. She only looked after their security as a by-product of keeping her rooms free of non-consensual violence. When the police cracked down on contraceptives following the controversy, she was asked to help find a way to supply them. She brought it up with Violet and they both decided that they were not prepared to take the risks associated with smuggling.

Mistigris was effectively a criminal. He was unable to legally acquire the metal and other equipment for his work because it was all controlled by the union. Had he asked Virginia's advice on the subject, she would have undoubtedly told him to pay lip service to the union and find a comfortable grey area between societal acceptance and subversion where he could continue to both work and live well. It was not his principles that kept him from doing this. He simply had no talent for it.

Violet believed that a certain amount of decay was healthy. It acted as a sort of fertilizer, like the urban waste that was shipped out to the market gardens around Provincetown. Over-fertilizing burned the roots and made life impossible. The strength of her conviction gave the impression that the words were not general commentary, but something more personal. The barren home life that led to her partnership with Virginia, and the various forms of prostitution that made the partnership work, certainly provided her with plenty of experience of the odd relationship between decay and health.

23

THE STATION AT THE OLD CEMETERY was small. It was an enclosed space that could only accommodate one two-car train with two platforms, one on each side. Sculpted concrete gave both platforms simple yet respectful detailing. The same plans were used for all the cemetery stations to save money and give mourners the impression the old and new cemeteries were essentially the same place. All of the buildings were converted into columbaria after the line was shut down. The one at Virginia's Theological Cemetery is on the walking tour, though there is nothing left that gives a sense of what it once was.

Since it was a separate line, they were able to use the newest electric technology. Each cemetery had a substation disguised as a crypt to provide power. The train was, comparatively speaking, quiet and efficient. Great pains were taken to not disturb people's grief.

The decision to install two platforms was an offshoot of these ideas. Caskets accompanied by family and friends, as well as people visiting graves, used one side. Unaccompanied caskets and everything else used the other. Early in the design process, the funeral industry asked that the trains be designed to transport headstones, maintenance equipment, personnel and whatever else they needed. The design team accommodated the request in such a way as to not interfere with the processions.

Once the lines were built between the cemeteries and the trains were in place, Virginia was invited to take a private tour. Violet, in contrast, could attend the official opening as her husband's plus one.

The engineer leading the tour referred to the train with such affection as the Death Train that Virginia was touched. Virginia asked the engineer if the casket segregation meant that the deceased were not equal on their way to their final resting place. The engineer replied that that was not the case. He explained that, given projected mortality rates, there would be ample room to lay caskets without crowding or stacking them, regardless of which platform was used. Equipment and all the rest would be the only things taking second place. In the letter to Violet describing the tour, Virginia noted her scepticism that the train would work that way in practice.

24

AFTER A BOTCHED BACKSTREET abortion took the life of one of the servers, Virginia asked Violet if they had made the right decision to limit helping the girls. Violet assured her that they were doing enough. Their business aided a lot of women who would be far worse off without safe and clean rooms to do what they needed to get by. It was the only moment I have found in my research when Virginia seemed genuinely concerned about others, without a hint of ulterior motives.

The moment did not last. It opened the door to speculation between the two women on how they would smuggle contraceptives and link clients to health care. They had no idea. Comparing Violet's circle of wives and the servers, it was clear that it came down to money and connections. Violet had access to services and would have no trouble making them available to Virginia. Expanding them to a larger—and poorer—group was practically unthinkable.

They concluded that the servers were already doing very well for themselves under the circumstances. As usual, Virginia avoided any hint that she did the same. If she did, she kept it to herself. If not, there would be no reason for other servers to think that she would be able to help them after the crackdown.

Since the train was fresh in their minds, the two women imagined how they would use it in their hypothetical smuggling operation. In certain ways, it seemed ideal. Police in the area were concentrated in Provincetown. Their main role was to be a visible presence on the more popular stages, which were all in the city. The stations had private platforms, making loading and unloading simple. The trains had ample room for miscellaneous items. Caskets were such a common sight around the old cemeteries that an extra one here and there would probably not be noticed.

The isolation of the new cemeteries was relative. There were towns in proximity. The train worked against the plan since very little road traffic went to the cemeteries. Virginia was convinced townspeople would notice the increased activity and would signal it to the authorities at the first inconvenience.

More fundamentally, neither Virginia nor Violet felt comfortable having a business relationship with the people who would make the products and deliver them to the train. As for abortions, they agreed that connecting them with cemeteries would just be tempting fate. Countless scenarios were imagined, but none were acted on.

25

THE FUNERAL INDUSTRY took a different view of the opportunities provided by the train. Land in the city was expensive. Many companies already had warehouses on the periphery, but that created transportation headaches. The new cemeteries, surrounded by cheap land and with built-in transportation to the heart of the city, were a dream come true.

They bought land in the towns. With the promise that warehouses would bring good jobs, they got permission to build them. It took another decade to move their manufacturing facilities and associated skilled labour. The buildings and activity are still there today, though they blend in with all the other industry built in the area after the ring road went through. It took about fifty years for Virginia's Theological Cemetery to completely lose its quiet, rural setting.

One of the councillors who frequented the hall kept Virginia informed about how the situation was evolving. Beyond the occasional snippet that fed into her and Violet's scenarios, she could not care less. The only concerns were with getting paid and not having to manage the land. She treated the topic as if it were anything the client was interested in, so, as far as the councillor knew, she was fascinated by the details.

She did mention to Violet that a pseudo-bohemian writer waxed on one evening about the poetry of it all. The Death Train, the writer claimed, was no different than Provincetown's anus. The city fed on people who willingly jumped into its gaping maw. It absorbed their energy until they were dried-up husks. Once there was nothing left, they were eliminated back into the countryside. The city was inefficient though; energy was always left over. Like the sewers that fertilized the market gardens, the corpses gave life to an industry.

The discussion turned around whether the city was the sort of entity that would soak up base energy. If it was effectively a higher form of collective life, perhaps it absorbed people's intelligence: their divine spark. One of the servers at the table asked if Violet's Deontological Necropolis would be an end in itself for the deceased that ended up going there, which caused the conversation to veer off in a new direction. Virginia was just amused that Violet was not the only one to make comparisons to market gardens.

26

ONCE PROVINCETOWN HAD ITS QUOTA of sculpted heroes of the Empire, the council turned its attention to the hall that hosted the yearly art exhibition. The developers of the Light and Air Program had not forgotten about their promise to the artists' union. More importantly though, they felt that the city needed another iconic building or two to be taken seriously as a cultural hub.

The council, in consultation with the Academy and the union, decided on a Renaissance Revival style. The style offered a good balance between tradition and forward-looking ideas. The detailing could be ornate enough to employ a large number of artists. There was also the option of carving out recesses and building projections to accommodate more sculptures.

Although more money and care was put into its construction than for housing in the poor neighbourhoods, this interpretation of a palace was not built to last. It was replaced about forty years later with Provincetown's second skyscraper, at an impressive twelve storeys.

The year before and several years after the palace was built marked the height of cooperation between the Academy and the union. They also felt an unmatched sense of self-importance that came from their association with such an illustrious building. As a result, their influence in respectable society was considerable.

They used their power to convince industrialists to handle their scraps with more care and have authorities take petty theft of materials more seriously. The intent was to stifle independent artists. Sculptors, since they needed more material than most other artists, were hit the hardest. Even easel painters felt the change, some turning to sketching and writing to get their ideas out.

27

MISTIGRIS STARTED TO COME to the concert hall more frequently after that. In an unguarded moment, he complained about having molds but nothing to fill them with. He was starting to gain a reputation in the local scientific community as someone who was doing interesting, innovative work. He actually had commissions to fill for the first time in his career. It was clear he thought if he could not deliver, he would fall further into poverty. The last half of the thought went unsaid, as far as I can tell.

Virginia wrote to Violet that Mistigris stood out at that moment from the usual mass of artists serving as supplementary entertainment. Violet dismissed his complaints as a clumsy ploy to get sympathy and free drinks. Still, as she was to a certain extent living vicariously through her partner, she asked for more details. Virginia replied that it was less what he was saying than the fact that he had taken on the characteristics of his graffiti. He looked soft, like solid wood losing its form to rot. She admitted the comparison wasn't perfect. It reminded her of the girls, ordinarily portraying the person their clients needed them to be with ease and confidence, caught short by decisions made by a callous society beyond their reach.

Neither Violet nor Virginia mentioned that a fair number of the hall's clients were in fact decision makers in respectable society and husbands of the women in Violet's circle. They did not question whether they themselves were callous in profiting from society's inequalities. Mistigris' misfortune was viewed more as a curiosity than an injustice.

Nonetheless, Virginia made a connection to the councillor's story about the Death Train and the funeral industry. The next time he was in the hall, she got him talking about headstones. He didn't know much; the industry was not well represented on council or in his social circles. He made an effort to sound knowledgeable anyway. In among the approximations and exaggerations he mentioned, accurately, that a transition was in the works from softer rock, like limestone, to the harder granite. Apparently, it was being driven by new carving methods.

Unlike contraceptives, stones were already being transported to and between cemeteries. Since it was completely legal, the people involved would probably be less suspicious or suspect. This did not make Virginia any more inclined to get into the smuggling business. It just added another scenario to the ongoing conversation. She also mentioned it to Mistigris in passing.

28

THE REACH OF MANY of the actresses and dancers on the formal stages of theatres and halls went farther. The men also expended their influence in society so that their mistresses would be cast in interesting and highly visible roles. These women were the admired and envied villains of Violet's circle.

The women were already partially accepted in respectable society. They knew their success rested in part on belonging to multiple spheres. Some genuinely liked it. None that I am aware of appreciated being on file with the vice squad as prostitutes. None liked that their performances on formal stages doubled as auditions for a private production. They weren't against private shows so much as the system that made them obligatory.

Building off the values that separated blatant sexuality from politics and instilled traditional sexual values in schoolchildren, they pushed for entertainment to be more family friendly. In private, the industrialists and bankers hated the idea. They frequented concert halls to escape the straightjacket of respectable society. In public, though, they could not afford to take an opposing view.

In a similar move to Virginia's in controlling and improving the bedroom, the women started to put money indirectly into productions on the formal stage. Exclusively male professions such as theatre owners and directors would not sign contracts with women who aspired to be more than objects on the stage. The women didn't want to turn to their protectors and risk betraying their ambition and independence. Instead, they found willing non-political anarchists who took a basic pleasure in the ruse.

The low-level campaign of persuasion was a success, if a slow, incremental one. Contracts where actors and dancers were paid more and more, eventually approaching a living wage, became the norm. Costumes became first a shared and then the complete responsibility of the production company. The goals were not achieved in the time period covered by this essay. Even in the early days however, the changes influenced Virginia's business.

29

MISTIGRIS' TIME AS A REGULAR at the concert hall was short-lived. The next time Virginia heard something about him worth writing down, it was by way of a rumour recounted by an unnamed pseudo-bohemian. According to the rumour, he had set up his workshop in the Death Train. From the bohemian's perspective, the unexpectedness of the move was in character for Mistigris. The creepiness of working around corpses fit well with the themes of decay and decline so evident in the artist's work. The workshop itself could even be seen as a sort of performance art, which was currently in vogue in the Capital.

The people around the table in the hall ultimately disapproved of it. For some, it was disrespectful to the dead. Others felt that the context was distasteful, amounting to a cheap, misguided spectacle. The commercial aspect was brought up, along with the question of whether he imagined the notoriety would make him more successful. Another suggested that the move was to ensure the very opposite, which would feed into his complex of being the marginalized artist.

Virginia was surprised by how far Mistigris had gone, but was even more taken aback by the hostility of the reaction. In her experience, industrialists and pseudo-bohemians alike enjoyed and encouraged offbeat creativity. They kept themselves at a safe distance and increasingly relied on the police to render it harmless. They spoke against it publicly. In a concert hall, however, they were generally more open. She did not mention that the suggestion to Mistigris to use materials from the funeral industry came from her.

In the letter describing the incident, she complained for the first time of feeling old. This became a regular sentiment in her correspondence with Violet up until the end. She seemed suddenly aware that she was no longer easily adapting to the world around her.

30

IT TURNED OUT THE RUMOURS shared around the table were true. Mistigris had set up his workshop in the Death Train. Contrary to much of the speculation, though, he had chosen his space purely for practical reasons. An interview in a new anarchist-leaning magazine, The Weekly Sedition, explored his thinking.

The joker sculptor had dismissed Virginia's idea at first. Stone would be even more unwieldly and heavier than metal. He couldn't gather scraps and melt them together afterwards. He couldn't work on a mold while collecting the scraps. Half of his work consisted of modifying the negative space of the mold. Stone needed to be sculpted directly, pulling out a form from an existing block.

Moving blocks to his workshop using his informal network would have been very difficult. Shifting the blocks in the small studio so he could get anything done would have been a nightmare. Getting his hands on the necessary tools, especially for harder rock, would have also been a challenge. He resorted to melting down the sculptures he was least satisfied with that littered his workshop.

In about the same measure that the funeral industry was disconnected from Provincetown's political elite, it was linked to Mistigris' friends and neighbours. No one was willing to help deliver material to him or risk allowing him to use company shops. Sculpting in the train was brought up as a joke, since responsibility for it was complicated.

As a rail line crossing local borders, it was under the authority of the Imperial Transportation Ministry. The authority was partially delegated to a syndicate made up of the City of Provincetown, the regional government that represented the rural area, and the railway consortium that built the line and was under contract to maintain it. The daily function was further delegated to Provincetown's Cemetery Operations Unit. The Unit, in turn, gave free rein to the industry for the transport of miscellaneous equipment and materials, so long as it did not detract unreasonably from the experience of mourners. The treatise on the Imperial Railway by Strunz is the best resource if you are curious to know more about the subject.

Mistigris took the idea of using the train seriously. His friends helped him find a job as a labourer and ensured that certain tools were accidently left in the car. He had to help load and unload on the unaccompanied casket platform. Other than that, he was free to do what he liked. The scientists and other enthusiasts of his work who followed his transition were responsible for picking up their sculptures at one of the cemeteries. They apparently found that added to the experience.

31

THE INCREASING RESPECTABILITY of the formal stages in concert halls and theatres slowly led to the whole establishment becoming respectable. Base prices for drinks and wages for servers were set. Servers could still earn more, using their charms for tips, but the charms that were acceptable and the increase in earnings were limited. The habit of sitting at a table with clients, selling their company as much as the alcohol, diminished. Instead, they wandered from table to table, taking and bringing orders with less and less interaction.

It was becoming unacceptable for a member of a group to disappear for a while with a server. With wages came the expectation that the server was always present and actually served. From the client's perspective, it was increasingly unseemly for servers to be prostitutes. Prostitutes had to be completely hidden, either in another, specialized establishment or in plain sight as companions who came with the group. For better or worse, the process of marginalizing prostitution that started with the decline of the Players and their houses of tolerance had taken another significant step.

Virginia's days as a server were coming to an end. She wrote to Violet that she was too old to be on her feet and be pleasant to strangers all day long. The need for rooms by the servers also dried up, so she was forced to reduce the number on hand. This was offset by the price she was able to charge for specialized rooms, both to higher end prostitutes and more adventurous couples and groups.

32

THE EMPIRE WAS ALSO FEELING its age. One of the jokes making the rounds in the Capital was that the Emperor had accepted his decline but was blind to his decay. It was said by people in respectable circles of the metropolis who knew nothing of Mistigris and little about his work. Yet it can be traced through the press— first mainstream, then anarchist—back to him. A political veneer to his usual themes was added by The Weekly Sedition and he was omitted as soon as it could stand on its own. His work suddenly became relevant, like a book cited by everyone but read by few.

Unlike the Players, the new councillors did not accept the limitations of their provincial stage. They had already shown a willingness to make noise on the main stage with the introduction of sex education and, more subtly, certain modifications to the Light and Air Program. Those efforts were informal, making the outcomes uncertain. The industrialists and bankers wanted more certainty, more transparency in decision making, and more people in government who understood their issues.

Symbolically, the sculpted heroes of the Empire were ever more disconnected from society. They were ancient history. Their strength made the current government seem weak. The appearance of weakness was magnified with the news of what other countries were accomplishing. The industrialists who controlled most of the newspapers hammered the innovation of other countries in order to push for change domestically.

The two other increasingly prominent voices called, respectively, for a return to the time of the sculpted heroes and for an acceleration of the process of decline and decay. Both were playing a long-running cat-and-mouse game with the police on the streets and parks in cities across the Empire. Claiming space with graffiti and other indirect methods transformed into marches and protests. Taking control of sidewalks evolved into occupying whole streets.

None of these movements resonated strongly with the general population. The Empire was relatively prosperous and quality of life had risen for most people. Health and jobs were what really counted, according to the most reliable studies, and there had been noticeable improvements in both domains in a generation. Security was a frequently raised concern, likely driving people away from the more disruptive groups. Politics as such was considered irrelevant, particularly outside the Capital.

33

VIRGINIA BECAME AN HONORARY figure in the hall. The owner knew she attracted councillors and other important people. She was also discreet about her less respectable activities. He encouraged her to turn a corner table into a sort of salon.

The pseudo-bohemians and the girls who ended up on the prostitute side of the server-prostitute profession faded away. They both migrated to the newly established suburbs, though suburbs that had very little in common with each other. The first was filled with scaled-down replicas of the upper-class houses with one owner from foundation to roof and a walled-in garden. The second were copies of the poor neighbourhoods in proximity to factories.

This created an awkward gap. Women could in theory frequent the hall without losing their respectability. In reality, many men still wanted to maintain a space away from the society their wives were a part of. They created a hostile environment for other women that Virginia was unable to counter. She found herself surrounded by men who talked politics, business and similar topics without the open-mindedness traditional to the hall. Lacking the playful yet cutting observations of the servers who used to sit at the table, the corner became an echo chamber.

Virginia wondered in a letter if things would be different if she weren't so old. Maybe then, she wrote, they wouldn't see her as a successful businessman who just happened to be wearing a dress. Violet responded by saying that at least she wasn't reduced to an item on the list a businessman needed to check off to consider himself successful, along with a house and an original piece of art. At least she was considered an independent person and not a ward of her husband.

The only women in the place were part of the anarchist crowd. The crowd was much younger and viewed Virginia's corner as a major obstacle to a better society. Without the servers and the enticement of cheap alcohol, the two groups did not mix. Virginia tried to engage with them but could not get past the inflexibility and what she considered the naiveté of their positions.

She opined to Violet that this was a generation who only knew the city and had never sacrificed to find a better life. Had they grown up in the countryside and moved to the city they would understand how difficult building a new life really was, and how rarely it lived up to utopian ideals. It troubled Virginia to see that they aimed to force everyone to make the sacrifice, and there was no limit to it. The new society envisioned by the anarchists would without a doubt be so much better that any and all sacrifice could be justified. It sounded to her like a cult.

Nonetheless, she was respectful and accommodating to them. Some even joined her in the corner when her usual circle was not around. They tried to convert her to their cause at first. Eventually the corner became an informal spot to chat about mundane and amusing things when they needed a break from planning their ideal world and the downfall of the current one.

34

OF ALL THE TOPICS that circulated in the corner, one of the most amusing was the eccentric sculptor who worked in the Death Train. The most recent story concerned a series of granite headstones he had carved for the graves of some of the unaccompanied caskets he shared a car with. The stones did not follow his usual themes of decline and decay, but rather manifested a simple strength and resilience. Mistigris' stones, incidentally, are part of my walking tour.

Asked to explain his ideas in The Weekly Sedition, he argued that cemeteries were enduring monuments to earthly decay. In the city, decay and decline were hidden. The inanimate was painted over and the living ordered to move on. In cemeteries, the healthy were confronted with the decomposition of beings that once were like them. Those still full of life then moved on, hid themselves from death in a maze of activity and creation.

The monument had reached an industrial scale though, like a mechanized farm. Visitors tended to only be moved by visible individual markers, representing only a fraction of humanity. Symbols resistant to decline into an undifferentiated grey background were necessary to signal to the living that more than what they chose to see in the city came to rest here.

The newspaper portrayed Mistigris as an engaged artist who fought against the injustices of society. The article underlined how ineffectual, if admirable, the effort was.

The rot in society had spread so deeply that it was no longer sufficient to simply draw people's attention to it. The only way to move forward was to tear down and replace the system. Once people were free from their predefined roles, they would come to appreciate all of humanity and not judge a life lived based on the quality of a headstone.

The notes from the interview suggest a different motive. In order to have enough room to work, Mistigris had to have the unaccompanied caskets stacked at one end of the car. He believed that the themes of decay and decline were already present in a cemetery, so his pieces could be limited to drawing attention to—as opposed to representing—them. At the same time, he felt guilty about mistreating bodies that nobody seemed to care about and would end up in relatively unadorned graves. It is just as likely that he carved the headstones to assuage his conscience as anything else.

35

ATTEMPTS TO MANIPULATE EVENTS and circumstances to serve political ends had become increasingly common by this time. One day, when the hall was mostly empty, Virginia was approached by one of the women from the anarchist crowd. The woman warned her that some in the group wanted to expose her less than respectable business, along with some of the local elite that took advantage of it.

Virginia was taken aback. Starting with the contraceptive controversy, the anarchists had made it clear that they were supportive of unrestricted expressions of human sexuality. The support covered deviance as much as it did health concerns. As opposed to the pseudo-bohemians, who opposed contraception as a way of keeping one foot in respectable society, the anarchists had tended to be more principled. While the former made sure that they would be accepted in the chic suburbs once they had had enough of bohemian life, the latter wanted to express what they believed was right.

She first thought that move was another way of putting hypocrisy on display. The elite had long felt free to pursue all sorts of sexual expression, then used the police to deny others what they themselves enjoyed, all in the name of morality. If the general public knew, Virginia supposed, maybe they would revolt against these and other forms of social control.

She was only half right. The anarchists had come against a wall of popular indifference they were having difficulty breaching. Some in the group felt that they needed to take a more active role in tearing down the Empire. They should blow up institutions, even assassinate leaders. It was foolish to believe that the public could understand that a better world was possible when they were being indoctrinated by these very institutions and leaders.

Another line of thought was to use the indoctrination for their ends. People had come to believe that everything beyond very basic sexual practices was immoral and odious. If they discovered the deviant activities their leaders partook in, perhaps they would turn against them. If done correctly, the temple would revolt against the palace and the people would tear down the Empire themselves.

This, Virginia discovered, was the motive behind exposing her business.

She thanked the woman for the warning and immediately wrote a message to Violet. Violet asked if there was anything they could do to stop it. The response was negative. The only thing to be done was to hunker down and wait for the storm to pass. Presumably Virginia passed the warning on to her clients, but, as one might expect, there is no record of it.

36

EVERY YEAR, PROVINCETOWN officials tried to entice notable people from the Capital to attend their exhibition of fine art. The palace replica provided a flash of interest that faded quickly. As with the art on display, connoisseurs were curious about the city's interpretation of the classics. Once it was found that the local fine art was essentially a less accomplished version of the offerings in the Capital, invitations were delegated downward.

The similarity meant that nothing negative could be said publicly about the Provincetown versions. That would reflect badly on the Capital's Academic art. But it would not do for the Capital to be unrepresented at the salon. The trick was to send the lowest person in the hierarchy possible without giving offense.

As the Provincetown anarchists experimented with new paths to revolution, a representative of the Provincetown Academy was presenting the salon's program to a minister in the Capital. In the representative's memoirs, he describes a "sinking feeling" as it became clear the minister was not paying attention and appeared to be half-asleep for much of the meeting. Dropping the names of the most celebrated local artists of the time made no difference. He became increasingly convinced some anonymous subordinate had been chosen to attend weeks before.

He wrapped up the pitch, thanked the minister for his time and started packing his plans and sketches. Then, suddenly, the minister asked him with some enthusiasm if "the decay and decline artist" would be there. Apparently, the decaying Emperor joke found its way to his ears and he was vaguely aware of its origin. The representative hesitated, then cautiously said that the work was not really Academic art but that something could be arranged. The minister nodded in reply.

37

THE UNION REFUSED TO SUPPORT sending an invitation to Mistigris. The Academy representative argued that, since the event was just around the corner, the sculptor would not have the time to create anything appropriate, so would likely decline the offer. They could claim to have made a reasonable effort to reach out to him. Mistigris' absence could only be blamed on his own intransigence.

The union believed that he would submit whatever happened to be lying around his studio. He would not be motivated to bring his best work to an event run by organizations that fought against his deviant art throughout his career. They feared Mistigris would try to discredit the show. Of course, even his best pieces would bring the exhibition into disrepute. Other artists might even withdraw their work.

The Academy retorted that the cohort of nameless subalterns the Capital was going to send already put the exhibition in disrepute. The benefit of having an Imperial minister in attendance more than made up for any damage an obscure artist might cause. So, an invitation was sent solely in the name of the Academy.

38

THE SCANDAL AROUND VIRGINIA'S business started out small, with an exposé appearing in several anarchist weeklies. It picked up steam when the industrialists who controlled the mainstream press decided the news damaged entrenched government interests more than theirs. They had also held the moral high ground since taking over the local council from the Players and were not about to cede it to the anarchists, whom they derisively termed a group of "baby nihilists."

The council directed the police to open an investigation into deviance in Provincetown. The investigation was set up as a general witch hunt. If random prostitutes in the eastern suburbs were picked up for solicitation or homosexuals for sodomy, the authorities could announce that progress had been made. It is clear in the case files that some of the city's most vulnerable groups took the brunt of the official response.

Virginia was questioned multiple times. Her only official income came from the cemetery leases, which was technically considered farm income. Violet's paranoia had rubbed off on her, so she kept a certain distance from the rooms. When she met with staff, it was typically in parks or halls she did not frequent rather than onsite in groups. Money circulated informally, which was generally accepted since most of her employees were women. People were under the mistaken impression that she was the force behind ensuring that there was equality in death, so that is what she focused on.

The notes from the interrogations reveal how good Virginia was at playing the part of a respectable and God-fearing woman. Officers in the room found her modest and respectful. She was a small-town girl without much education who struggled in the city. Despite the loss of innocence that came with cleaning rooms in a brothel and serving alcohol in bars and concert halls, she had never lost sight of God. When an opportunity arose to contribute her inheritance for the good of the community, she did not hesitate. The possibility that she had secured the money to buy the land, as opposed to inheriting it, was so far beyond what they considered possible that they did not bother to check how she came to own it. It was outrageous that a person so devoted would be accused of being the handmaiden of abject vice.

At the same time, the police were convinced she was guilty. They had testimony from former servers who ended up as suburban prostitutes, given in exchange for dropping solicitation charges. She could also be connected to several known deviants. There was no direct evidence however. Because of the warning, Virginia had suspended activities before the scandal blew up. They hoped she would slip up under questioning, but it didn't happen. Given the sensitivity and weakness of the case, they decided not to charge her.

She was nonetheless accused, tried and convicted in the media, simply to drum up as much moral outrage as possible. Her salon in the hall was lost. After a discussion with Violet about fighting back, they decided their current strategy of hunkering down was still the best. The accusations were not far from the truth. Conflict would prolong the exposure and increase the chance that somebody would find something solid.

The anarchists were successful in increasing the sense of decay and decline. The media attention shone a spotlight on groups the virtuous residents of Provincetown had convinced themselves only existed in the Capital. The anarchists were unable to keep control of the story though, so it is unclear that the scandal furthered their cause. If anything, people were holding on ever tighter to what they had.

39

MISTIGRIS RECEIVED THE INVITATION a week before the exhibition. His initial thought, according to what he told a journalist at the event later, was that he could get access to previously unattainable materials. He had sketches for metal sculptures he still wanted to create. Then he looked closer and realized the union stamp was missing.

It was only at that point that he paid attention to the event itself. The invitation seemed backwards. Typically, artists submitted specific pieces. If the piece was judged worthy, it was included. There were sometimes whole rooms dedicated to one person, but they were invariably dead. He would not have been surprised if high ranking members of the Academy and union were allowed to display whatever they wanted, but that did not explain the situation at hand.

In the end, he decided that it did not matter. He asked the journalist if he believed the invitation was important. The journalist replied that it was without precedent. Non-affiliated artists had been invited to contribute in the past, but only on condition of membership. Mistigris' inclusion could shift the very definition of art, properly speaking. Mistigris concluded that his presence was therefore meaningless and then wandered off, leaving the journalist in the lurch.

It seemed to be a foregone conclusion that he would participate. He never expressed any doubt as to what work to put on display or worry about the lack of time to prepare. There was no explanation for why he believed his participation to be insignificant.

40

THE LETTERS BETWEEN Virginia and Violet had become less frequent and more generic. They just checked in and made sure the line of communication stayed open. They might have also thought that stopping outright would look suspicious, if anyone was paying attention.

The police had made a connection to Violet's world. Testimony for some of the former servers included room locations. "Respectable lady" and "gentleman" came up multiple times in descriptions neighbours gave, along with vague details that only narrowed down age and general style. Even though Virginia's cleaning and security staff visited the rooms far more often than clients, the neighbours did not appear to notice them. They were just as invisible when they carted off the fetish equipment.

The casefiles did not give a sense that the officers knew exactly who was involved or in what capacity. They were inclined to ascribe the visits to affairs. While adultery was technically deviant behaviour, it was evidently not what they were looking for.

41

WHILE THE TWO WOMEN made themselves scarce, Mistigris had taken centre stage. Reporters did not particularly care about his work. They were mostly interested in the personality of an artist who was able to make a living, however marginal, outside of the artistic establishment. The mainstream press dismissed him as a curiosity, a "poster child for the accomplishments of anarchism" who could barely feed himself, let alone run a bank or a factory. Readers had the luxury to indulge his eccentricities because of the responsible, practical people in society who created prosperity for everyone.

The anarchist press used him as a representative of their

movement. Turning his back on the obsolete institutions of the Empire did not end with dying in the gutter. He was not only able to feed himself and put a roof over his head, he was accomplished and respected in his field. Otherwise, the thinking went, he would not have been invited to a prestigious exhibition. The risks of getting rid of the Empire were in reality opportunities to flourish.

The nostalgic papers argued for the return of strong leadership to shepherd the flock. Mistigris, they explained, did not purposefully seek to create chaos. He was just lost and needed a firm hand to bring him back into the fold. If he kept going astray, he should be permanently separated from the group. It wasn't his fault, but the danger he posed to others who might inadvertently follow him had been criminally underappreciated.

After the initial rush of journalists, interaction became awkward. Nobody could find the work Mistigris was supposed to have put on display. Because of the strange, last minute invitation, nobody knew what to look for. At the same time, nobody felt comfortable asking him, since others might take the question for a sign of interest. Not even the Academy artists were willing to risk that sort of stigma.

42

RISK AVERSION WAS A MAJOR THEME of the exhibition. While none of the artists were willing to speak to Mistigris, there are multiple accounts of what they had to say amongst themselves. Ordinarily, once the exhibition catalogue was published, Provincetown's elite started speculating as to which pieces had the potential of becoming tomorrow's masterpieces. Many artists would receive offers to purchase their piece in the time leading up to the event. This year, there was only one offer.

Neither the Academy nor the union were involved in the deals.

They regulated calls, style and materials, but encouraged a laissez-faire approach to most sales. A work needed to be considered a masterpiece on the open market to be a masterpiece in the eyes of the world. The optimal result for the two organizations was for art to both follow their rules and be judged independently as brilliant.

The problem was that local buyers did not really believe that the works would ever be considered brilliant, but were willing to take the chance if the price was right. Inherent value and personal taste were not factors in the decision. Token investment in the local scene probably was, though evidently not an important one.

The income from selling exhibited pieces was on the other hand important for the artists. They had criticized the masterpiece system in the past as it reduced the work to its base commercial value. The system was accepted however, since it gave them the means to continue to create. It also allowed many of them to dream of striking it rich one day, although they were sometimes loathe to admit it.

The recent exposure of Provincetown's moral decay, added to the generally recognized notion that the Empire's glory days were behind it, lowered the risk the investors were willing to accept. Purchases of art in general had become less frequent. When local speculators did buy, they preferred foreign art from countries and schools with better pedigrees. As for the few foreign speculators interested in the Empire, Provincetown was almost always overlooked in favour of the Capital.

43

IN THE EVENING, ONE OF THE GUESTS from the Capital finally posed the question to Mistigris. The official was not nearly as concerned about stigma as the Provincetown community. More than that, he was both irritated and bored. Conversation after conversation centred around how morally upstanding Provincetown was. Locals boasted about how the last pockets of deviance in the city were being eradicated at that very moment. It was not-so-subtly implied that the Capital was a cesspool.

Since we only have the perspective of the official, it is impossible to tell how insufferable the Provincetown crowd actually was. The man definitely liked to be entertained, which included the company of women. His expectations were a throwback to the time of the houses of tolerance, when politics and pleasure mixed. From his perspective, the art on display was no more pleasing than wallpaper, which would have only been acceptable if the foreground was more agreeable.

Mistigris invited him outside to look at the palace's façade. In every niche, he had managed to have the statues replaced by his pieces. As was his habit, he had submitted projects in response to the calls sent out when the hall was transformed into a palace. Despite the predictable rejections, he had apparently gone ahead and finished many of them. With only a week's notice to produce something, that work became the most practical choice.

The façade was being touched up before the event in an effort to give visitors the best impression possible. Mistigris must have found some sympathetic craftsmen to help him with the installation.

His work was typically striking because of the unanticipated juxtaposition of decay and permanence. In this case, people saw— and expected to see—an elaborate façade. Regardless of the specific themes, the pieces just blended into the embellishment. The most notable impression was how this shift from unexpected to expected altered the impact of the work.

The official appreciated taking the local pretention down a notch, but was ultimately unmoved. Everyone had already accepted that the Empire was well past its prime. Groups across the political spectrum were in the middle of a game of one-upmanship, denouncing the rot and selling their miraculous cure with ever increasing spectacle. The decaying Emperor joke was already tame and Mistigris' art predated it. The minister had not come. The only solution as far as the official was concerned was to try to find a spot in the benighted town where entertainment had not been completely choked out.

Mistigris' statues, along with all the other salvageable pieces of the palace, were stored in a government warehouse when the building was demolished. Requests can be made to the municipal archivist to view them.

44

SOON AFTER THE EXHIBITION, Violet passed away. The official report lists the cause as an accident in the home. She had slipped and hit her head. Her husband was in the house at the time and was the sole witness. No other information was included.

Unlike Virginia, Violet was buried in her titular necropolis. Strangely, the headstone is clearly the work of Mistigris. It is the only one of his headstones I have been able to find for an accompanied casket, let alone one that replaced an already existing stone.

The records indicate the original stone had an inscription describing her as a wife and mother. The replacement stone describes her as an entrepreneur, dedicated mother and dear friend. It was clearly arranged by Virginia.

If you will allow me to fill in the blanks with speculation, Violet's husband may have become suspicious of her role in the business. Perhaps someone involved in the investigation mentioned something and he was able to put everything together. Perhaps someone in Violet's circle let something slip. Perhaps Violet herself tipped him off. She could have been acting differently if the investigation was making her anxious or paranoid. In any case, the revelation could have led to an argument that turned violent.

If Violet's description of her home life in her correspondence is accurate, her husband was a cold and distant man. They barely saw each other. She never gave any indication that he was violent or that she suffered physical abuse, and she was not shy about criticizing him. So perhaps my speculation is unfounded, and it was just an unfortunate incident sparked by so many secrets coming to light all at once.

Virginia knew her friend felt that marriage was a prison. She was the ward of her husband, who kept her poor and powerless. Despite this handicap, she managed find a way to thrive. As time went on, the letters reflected a person who defined herself less by her disappointments and frustrations. Instead, she embodied her accomplishments.

By the end, I think it is fair to say that her marriage was no longer a defining characteristic of her life. It just happened to be the reason she was in the ground. Following Mistigris' logic, the headstone should be a counterpoint—perhaps even the contradiction—to what was underneath.

45

IT WAS JUST A MATTER OF TIME before violence broke out across the Empire. When a bomb went off in one of the Death Train cars, people were more surprised at the choice of target—an obscure train in Provincetown—than the fact of a bombing. The anarchists were both blamed and took credit for the act. The records are however inconclusive. At least a dozen books have been written on the subject, each arguing fairly convincingly that different groups and individuals, both domestic and international, were responsible.

The bomb went off on the accompanied side. The car was filled with the mourners for a distant relative of a senior but unimportant member of the Imperial entourage. He died along with fifteen other people. Mistigris and the engineer were the only other people on the train. Mistigris broke one of his legs in multiple places when a headstone fell on it. The engineer suffered cuts and bruises.

The venue for the explosion was too isolated for the population to feel touched by the incident. Many people had used the train, but only in the setting of a death ritual. The incident was soon turned into a joke. The victims were after all halfway to the grave already. The expression "Death Train" took on greater popularity, in the sense of being "a convenient place to expire."

The contractor responsible for the upkeep of the train had it running again in a week. Since the car was too damaged to be repaired, it was simply replaced. Security was marginally increased when a worthy enough audience was present. The central purpose of the police was still to be a visible presence, so the train could never be considered a priority. The steady stream of the dead soon continued as if nothing had happened.

Many critics viewed the attack as an important point in Mistigris' evolution. They argued that his thematic range expanded from playing the resilience of life in the neighbourhood off the decay of that environment, to contrasting the permanency of death with transitory decline. Mistigris however had always found such distinctions artificial, lending themselves more to manifestos than art.

Regardless of how natural decay and decline may have been, they were constantly assisted by people's conscious decisions. The collapse of the building in his old neighbourhood was no less deliberate and just as much a tragedy. He thought that the train was chosen mainly because it was such an easy target and added nothing new to the sense of tragedy. The only noticeable effect was the variety of materials he began to use once he got his hands on the condemned car.

46

ON A WALKING TOUR, I occasionally point out locations where something happened or somebody lived but no trace is left. The event or person must be of particular interest to the audience, though, and it has to be well documented. I have taken more liberty here with Virginia's life. There has nonetheless always been something on which to base my speculations.

After Violet's headstone, there is a significant gap in the records. I am tempted to say something in any case, just to keep the sense of narrative going. I will say that Virginia was still alive.

Prostitution bounced back after the initial effort to stamp out vice. The press moved on to other things and the police returned to a more pragmatic approach. It is difficult to track the supply of rooms for the purposes of prostitution, but it appeared to have gradually re-established itself as well. The ideas used were no longer new, so the days of Virginia and Violet's monopoly was over.

The incremental improvements led by entertainers and producers continued to make their stages more respectable. Police harassment of women on sidewalks declined. The world was moving along without Virginia.

47

IMPERIAL FUNDING FOR ART fell off when the government ran out of prominent places to put the works. For sculptures, the rule was to have one major piece per square, visual endpoint to a street, or lobby. Easel paintings were generously spaced out on walls, so as to not detract from their individual importance. Rotating the works was discouraged in order to maintain the impression of permanence. Building façades that deserved to be enriched artistically were rare. The Capital held out longer than other cities, since most institutions were located there, but still ended up seeing a decline.

The failure of the masterpiece system and the lack of public support triggered a revolt among union membership. Both government and business interests took the position that the creation of art was an end in itself. Artists, it was felt, were free to derive an income through their work, but only in a market-driven context. In that case, the work was just an ordinary product and not really art. Anyone who felt deserving of payment should stop calling themselves an artist, hand in their union card and take a job in industry.

In the Empire, art had been held up as an enduring social good. That was what justified the central control for both Academic and religious art. The ministry responsible, and therefore the Provincetown Council, interpreted "social good" as the promotion of their interests, which they saw as identical to those of the country. Nonetheless, unlike countries with more individualistic leanings, there was already a culture of artistic creation serving other aims.

Just as the Academic revolt that created the union kept much of the principles intact, this revolt fell well short of a revolution. The leadership was replaced by long-time members. Their plan was to lobby industry and government for more support.

48

UNION INNOVATION STARTED with opening up membership in order to increase both the number of artists and the breadth of skills they represented. Despite some residual resistance reflected in meeting minutes, even Mistigris was accepted.

The second move was to deal directly with any ministry that would talk to them. At that time, the ministry responsible was the Ministry of Culture. Their mandate was to safeguard and advance Imperial culture. Practically, that meant reproducing it.

A breakthrough came with the Ministry of Health, which wanted to put out an information campaign to deal with an uptick in cases of syphilis. The basic message would be that blindness could be avoided if a doctor was consulted early enough. The message needed to reach people efficiently and inexpensively, so easel painting was dropped in favour of modern printmaking. Realism made way for abstracted forms and prominent text.

Printmaking was an already established practice but it was not formally considered art. This change allowed for broader expression on the artistic side and increased technical innovation. The quality ended up being better and the posters had more impact.

The next ministry the union worked with was Correctional Services. They wanted to start a pilot project of painting murals in prisons to reduce violence. Strangely, given the themes of his previous work, Mistigris painted one of them. He commented that it felt like he was kid again painting graffiti. Unfortunately, the project ended after the pilot. The murals were painted over several years later and no pictures of them survive.

49

THE BOMB ON THE DEATH TRAIN divided the anarchists. Some believed that the group had to go further to hasten the decline of the Empire. Others were somewhere between troubled and horrified by the reality of killing people, even if they were not against it in theory. Although other bombings and assassinations were planned, the group now lacked the cohesion to pull them off.

Violence shifted to suppressing worker organisation by the industrialists, aided by the police, and attacks of migrants and minorities by those nostalgic for the glory days of the Empire. Quality of life was noticeably slipping as economic growth had slowed and the deterioration of the infrastructure built through the Light and Air Program continued. Despite this, there was no existential threat to the system.

Stability was not enough for the government. They needed the strength, or at least the appearance of strength, to ensure that the country would not be a target for its more youthful and vigorous neighbours. One change was rebranding of the Ministry of Defense as the Ministry of War.

By this time, union artists had followed the syphilis campaign with several other successful programs. Because of this, the decision was made to accompany the rebranding with an extensive propaganda push. Soon, the Ministry of War was the largest employer of artists in the country.

Studies show that the propaganda influenced people's sense of security and confidence in the government. For Mistigris, it was off-putting. In his mind, such a grand effort to show fortitude had to cover an equal measure of decay and decline. In line with his usual principled practicality, he chose to emigrate.

50

I FOUND THE LETTERS between Virginia and Violet in the catalogue of the library in what was likely Virginia's home town under "uncatalogued." In the same file was an unpublished, undated obituary:

Virginia was a fallen woman. She was too innocent to resist the siren call of the city and slowly drowned in its vice. She left a part of herself behind in the countryside, uncorrupted. As she was slipping away, she transformed that portion into an island of final rest. She used her base influence to have a link created between terrestrial vice and heavenly virtue. The so-called Death Train was misnamed, as it led to eternal life. She provided a refuge in death for the redeemable who lived in the heart of modern sin.

Virginia was not among them. She was too deeply penetrated by spiritual sickness to accept extreme unction. She passed away a lewd degenerate in the service of God.

A library was established after the town received a gift from an anonymous donor. Since then, it has received half the money from the new cemeteries lease. A town about the same distance from Violet's Deontological Necropolis receives the other half. The intent of the donations in public record was to provide the means for independent study, particularly for those who had limited access to formal education.

Since the legitimate income from the cemeteries is partially public, we know that the money went to a notary public during Virginia's lifetime. Given average life expectancy, many years passed between her death and the arrangement for the libraries, when the money was still going to the notary. If the library and papers did in fact end up in her home town, then the missing link is likely Louise. She was the only person we know of who was familiar with Virginia's business and came from the same town.

None of this is certain. Perhaps Virginia did have children, raised outside her world of vice. They might have only learned of her real life through the papers the notary gave them, mixed in with their mother's effects. They may have been shocked and repulsed by how their inheritance had been earned. So they disposed of it in a way that might give women a sense of the world before they moved to the city.

Unless Virginia had a complete change of personality, the libraries were probably not her idea. She simply did not help others unless there was a connection with her own business interests. She probably would have burned the letters before they became public record and ended up being used in an essay like this.

AFTERWORD

In his argument for where to place Ernst Neizvestny in history, Berger talked about old and new heroes. Heroes are people who demonstrate courage. Up until recently, the demonstration was almost invariably "by deliberately risking their lives." All the statues in the streets of Provincetown followed this model.

The anarchists who likely put a bomb in the Death Train thought of themselves as misunderstood heroes. Only once their ideal society came to fruition would they truly be recognized. They were willing to be executed to hasten the downfall of the Empire. In the mainstream press, they were considered cowards because they were a safe distance away when the bomb exploded. They killed while avoiding a direct threat to their own lives.

The nostalgics had similar ideas as the anarchists. They yearned for a time of heroes so that they could risk their lives. The decline of the Empire was directly linked to leaders too cowardly to make hard decisions and be willing to pay the ultimate price for them. Their compromises led to domestic indifference and emboldened enemies beyond the borders. The decision to install the statues was blatant hypocrisy.

The Ministry of War propaganda took the same path. It appealed to people's vanity in the guise of courage. Foreign enemies were at the gates. The Emperor needed you, as an individual citizen and patriot, to arise and prepare yourself for the upcoming battle. "War" was never used, since the word implied a longer engagement that included more marching and other drudgery than moments of individual bravery.

Berger argued that the ideal crumbled in the face of advances in mass killing, both in war and peacetime. The First World War marked the definitive turning point. Now, the anonymous millions must fight or resist on a continuous basis. "Today the hero is ideally the man who resists without being killed."

I would add that advances in marketing have kept the old ideal alive precisely because it is no longer effective. While the residents of Provincetown turned their back on the statues and the calls of the anarchists and nostalgics, they were taken in by the efforts of the Ministry of War. The dream of being a singular hero distracted from resistance to the slow process of decline and decay.

At the centre of the old notion of heroes was "freedom as an individual privilege." It was an individual who chose to risk their life, and a statue of one person that was created to commemorate the fact. Yet it is groups—nations, classes, races, sexes—that are exploited or subservient today. It is unreasonable to suggest that the group should choose to risk extermination. If courage is survival and resistance however, the choice makes more sense.

Neizvestny and his art represented for Berger this new heroism, which is neither individualistic nor a courtship with death. The art engages with death, but in a fashion that emphasises the persistence of life in the face of adversity. It uses individual human figures without glorifying individual accomplishment.

Berger was confident that the struggle for human freedom would come to a positive end. It would take time and would be far from easy, but it would be successful. Though there is no evidence that Neizvestny had such grand intentions, his work was an "interim monument" to the struggle. This is significant because it is a monument to rejecting the current state of affairs. Since there are no excuses left for poverty, famine, exploitation, or anything of the sort, the only alternative to rejection is to renounce our humanity. Berger uses stronger language: we would be choosing to commit suicide as human beings.

Neither Virginia nor Mistigris accepted the world in which they found themselves. Virginia, along with Violet, was part of a group whose freedom had been limited for quite some time. Given the circumstances of her death, Violet resisted but likely died because of it. Virginia survived and arguably made a difference, if not a monumental one.

It could be argued that other women, such as those who took control of the formal stages in concert halls, made more of a difference. That is not important with the new definition of heroism; it only matters that they made a difference, not that they were the one to carry the day.

Mistigris is closer to Neizvestny, as they were both non-conformist sculptors who preferred large, public works. They were both rejected by artists' organizations that promoted cultural inertia. Their obsessions—the first with decline and decay, the second with death—were not all that different. Mistigris was labelled an anarchist, Neizvestny a nihilist. For Berger, Mistigris might qualify as a modern hero.

Intentionality is a problem here. Once a work of art has been released into the world, it can be interpreted freely, regardless of the intention of the artist. Berger however takes one step further. He states that the artist "is the example of a man, and it is his art that exemplifies him." So, the interpretation of the art becomes that of the artist.

If the art represents enduring struggle, a struggle that will lead to a better world, then the artist does too. He becomes the model of resistance without death—a modern hero. Other people, who might find the art opaque or grotesque, can still appreciate and emulate the artist. They cannot however leave the artist to be their champion, because modern heroism is ultimately a question of everyone in the group finding and exercising their freedom.

Throughout his career in Provincetown, various political groups either claimed Mistigris as their own or tried to demonize him with one label or another. He was socially conscious and was an anarchist insofar as he preferred informal, unlayered relationships with others. Like Neizvestny, he was also pragmatic in finding buyers for his work. There is some room to describe them politically, but the description must be balanced with personal obsessions and other aspects of their characters.

It seems to me that positing either of them as an antagonist to world-scale imperialism and a monument of resistance on the path to Berger's post-exploitation society goes too far. I would say that the person painting them with that brush has spent too much time in Virginia's Theological Cemetery. They would benefit from taking a trip on the Death Train to Violet's Deontological Necropolis.

I write walking tours. I failed out of my graduate program because the fiftieth primary source that I just had to get to justify my argument was too much. I have been known to embellish my anecdotes from time to time, just to make things more interesting for whoever happened to walk all that way. It is difficult not to admire the passion and vision behind the drive to a world without exploitation.

Despite running a business that profited from inequality and acting ungenerously most of the time, Virginia Antelme could be considered a hero. Many young women fresh off the train would have ended up on the street without her. Those who became prostitutes could at least ply their trade in relative cleanliness and security. She may not fit into the grand narrative of resistance and survival, but I hope the reader recognizes, as I have, that she is no less worthy of being remembered.

Trent Portigal is a writer of political tales and urban anecdotes. His second novel, *A Floating Phrase*, was shortlisted for the Robert Kroetsch City of Edmonton Book Prize. Trent spends his days planning cities on the Canadian prairies. He lives in Edmonton, Canada.